The Light Sprites

Written By
Lauren Page

Illustrated By
Dylan Hassell

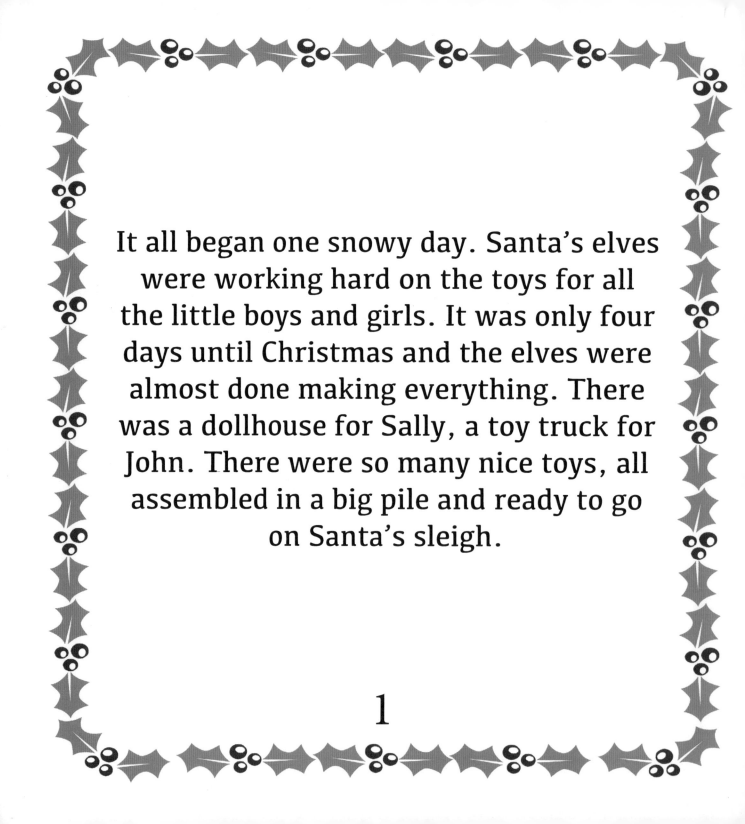

It all began one snowy day. Santa's elves were working hard on the toys for all the little boys and girls. It was only four days until Christmas and the elves were almost done making everything. There was a dollhouse for Sally, a toy truck for John. There were so many nice toys, all assembled in a big pile and ready to go on Santa's sleigh.

1

2

Soon enough, it was here. It was finally Christmas Eve. Santa got on his sleigh, ready to start delivering gifts to all the little boys and girls around the world.

4

As Santa left the North Pole, Mrs. Claus and all the little elves behind, he shouted, "Ho, Ho, Ho!"

6

The snow was getting heavy as Santa rode on his sleigh through Maine. "Whoa, ho, ho!" he said to himself as he looked down below the thick clouds to see where the traffic lights were.

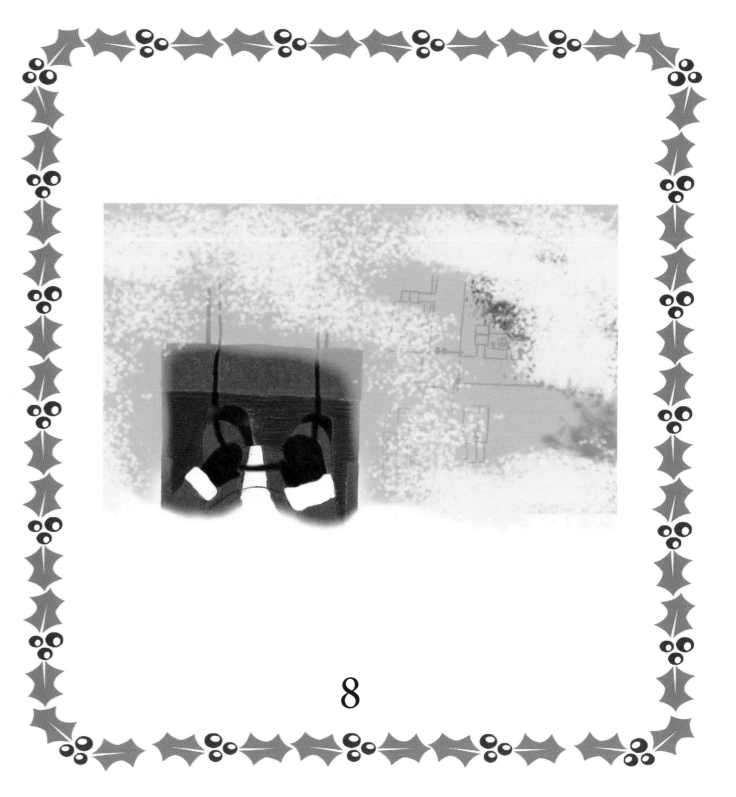

8

He was eventually able to deliver all the presents for all the good boys and girls, but with too many obstacles. When he returned to the North Pole where the elves and Mrs. Claus were waiting patiently, he told everyone what had happened.

10

"I couldn't find the lights," he explained, "I almost had to come back and call off Christmas! Thankfully I had remembered where the rest of the houses in Maine were, since that was my last stop."

12

For the next few days, the elves couldn't stop thinking about what Santa had told them. Mrs. Claus had an idea. "What if you guys volunteer to keep the lights lit?" she asked. "Maybe you could help all year long! It'll make the sky safer for Santa Claus and keep the roads safer for everyone else!"

14

"You know what, Mrs. Claus?" shouted Fern, a very handy elf, "That's a great idea! I'll go tell the big guy right now!"

16

So Fern ran off and told Santa about what the elves and Mrs. Claus were thinking. "Ho, Ho, Ho! Fern! Did you come up with this great plan?" asked Santa. Fern answered, "No, Mr. Claus. Actually, your wife did, sir."

18

"Ho, Ho, Ho! Well, Fern, please tell Mrs. Claus thank you for the great idea! Say, would you like to be the green light in the most important traffic light?" asked Santa.

20

"Oh boy, would I!" exclaimed Fern. "I'd love to! But Mr. Claus...what's the most important traffic light for? Where will it be?"

22

"Why, here at the North Pole!" answered Santa. "It'll come in handy up here for when I take off and land every Christmas Eve. It'll also help for when Mrs. Claus and I go on those vacations to Hawaii!"

24

"Then who will be in charge of the yellow and red lights in the most important traffic light?" asked Fern.

"Why, none other than Goldie and Ruby!" Santa responded. "They're perfect for the job. They're just as hard-working as you and their names even match the job description!" Santa winked.

28

When Fern returned to tell Mrs. Claus and the other elves the good news, everyone was excited to get to work. "The best part is, we get to work with our friends all year long!" exclaimed Fern.

30

"But what should we call our traffic light team?" asked Goldie. It was a good question. Elves were known as the helpers for Christmas, not traffic light monitors.

32

"How about the light sprites?!" shouted Ruby. "That's perfect. Let's get to work, light sprites!" said Fern, and on that note, they all set off to their traffic lights to start their new journey together.

34

35

The End

The Light Sprites

Text © 2014 by Lauren Page

Illustrations © 2014 by Dylan Hassell

The text for this book is set in Kefa.

The illustrations for this book are rendered in pen, colored pencil, and colored digitally using Adobe Photoshop.

Published by Create Space.

ISBN-13: 978-1500324025

ISBN-10: 1500324027

37

Made in the USA
Columbia, SC
13 October 2017